LILY
TO THE rescue

ALSO BY W. BRUCE CAMERON

# W. BRUCE CAMERON

# LILY
## TO THE rescue

Illustrations by

## JENNIFER L. MEYER

**A TOM DOHERTY ASSOCIATES BOOK**

**NEW YORK**

LILY TO THE RESCUE

Copyright © 2020 by W. Bruce Cameron
Illustrations © 2020 by Jennifer L. Meyer

Designed by April M. Ward

A Starscape Book
Published by Tom Doherty Associates
120 Broadway
New York, NY 10271

www.tor-forge.com

The Library of Congress Cataloging-in-Publication Data
is available upon request.

ISBN 978-1-250-23435-3 (trade paperback)
ISBN 978-1-250-23434-6 (hardcover)
ISBN 978-1-250-23430-8 (ebook)

Our books may be purchased in bulk for promotional, educational, or business use. Please contact your local bookseller or the Macmillan Corporate and Premium Sales Department at 1-800-221-7945, extension 5442, or by email at MacmillanSpecialMarkets@macmillan.com.

First Edition: March 2020

Printed in the United States of America

0  9  8  7  6  5  4  3  2  1

*Dedicated to my dog Tucker,*

*who loves his tiny piece of cheese.*

LILY
TO THE rescue

y name is Lily, and I have a lot of friends.

My best friend of all, of course, is Maggie Rose.

In the nighttime, I sleep on Maggie Rose's bed, pressed up against her warm legs. I get to lie there until Mom or Dad pokes a head in the doorway and says the word *school*.

Maggie Rose will groan a little, and then she climbs slowly out of bed and puts on her

clothes and goes into the kitchen for breakfast with her brothers. While she's chang-
ing clothes, I lie on the bed, missing her legs
and trying to show her that we would all be
happier if she just climbed back under the
covers.

But she never does that on days people say
*school.* I don't know why.

I think school must be a place, because
one day when Mom said *school,* Maggie Rose

let me ride in the back seat of the car with her. We went to a room with many children her age sitting in chairs. I sat next to Maggie Rose at the front of the room so that everyone could admire what a good dog I could be. I am very good at sitting.

Maggie Rose said, "Hello. My name is Maggie Rose Murphy. I live in Golden,

Colorado. I am in the third grade. My father is a game warden for the state of Colorado, and my mother works in animal rescue. She's a veterinarian. My dog's name is Lily."

When she said my name, I looked up at Maggie Rose and wagged. I did not know what we were doing, but all the children were looking at us, and it made me feel very important.

"Lily is a rescue dog for two reasons," Maggie Rose continued. I wagged again. "The first reason is that she was taken in by the shelter where my mom works, so she was rescued. And the second reason is that most days she goes back to the shelter to take care of all the animals there."

Maggie Rose started smiling and speaking a little more quickly. "Lily plays with the other dogs and helps them relax and not feel scared. She plays with the cats, too. She loves cats! Sometimes she curls up with the kittens and they sleep together. It helps because then the kittens don't grow up to be scared of dogs, and they can get adopted into families with dogs."

She paused and took a deep breath.

"So Lily has a job—a job in animal rescue. On weekends, I sometimes help at the

shelter, too. It's good for the puppies or kittens to get used to kids. Then they're not nervous around us."

"Lucky!" one of the children moaned.

I wagged some more. It just seemed like a good idea.

"I have two brothers," Maggie Rose went on. "One is named Bryan, and he is in fifth grade. One is named Craig, and he is in eighth grade. When I grow up, I want to be a veterinarian. When Craig grows up, he wants to be a baseball player. And I don't think Bryan will ever grow up."

For some reason, all the children laughed when Maggie Rose said this even though I had not done anything special. Sometimes people laugh just because they are happy there is a dog in the room.

"My name is Maggie Rose Murphy, and that is my report," Maggie Rose said. Everyone clapped because I was doing such a good job doing Sit. Then all the children lined up and took turns petting me, which was very nice. Maggie Rose gave me a treat, and that was even nicer.

That was an unusual day. On most days when somebody says *school,* I don't get to go to that place with all the children and the treats. Instead, Maggie Rose leaves after breakfast, and I go to Work.

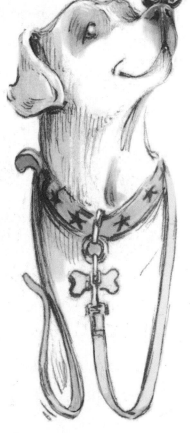

Work is a place just like school is a place. I go there with Mom. There are good treats at Work, and there are also friends: dogs, cats, and other animals in cages. The dogs and cats and the rest of the animals stay at Work for a while and then leave with happy people. I am the only dog who goes to Work and then goes home and goes back again the next day. That makes me special.

I like Work days, even though Maggie Rose gets out of bed before I am ready for her to do that. But the days when nobody says *school* and when I don't go to Work are even better.

Then I can spend the whole day with my girl, Maggie Rose. And sometimes we go to the dog park!

The dog park is the most wonderful place I have ever been. Even better than bed with Maggie Rose's warm legs. Even better than Work, where there are friends and treats.

At the dog park, there are dogs, squirrels, birds, and children. I do not know if all the dogs are there all the time or if they just make sure to be there when I arrive.

I am friends with every-
one at the dog park, except
the squirrels. It really isn't
possible to make friends with
squirrels, because they always
run away. I have tried, and it just
doesn't work.

One day at the dog park, I made a
new friend.

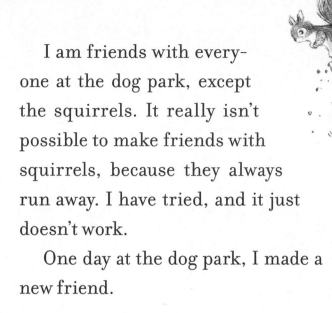

There are some important rules in the dog park. First, one dog should never take a toy away from another dog. Dogs don't like that. People can take away toys if they want, because they are people. The rule doesn't apply to people.

Next, a dog should always politely sniff another dog in the butt. If you don't sniff a dog, it is considered to be very rude. (This rule does not apply to people, either.)

When Maggie Rose first lets me into the dog park, I love to run and run and run. I will wag and bow and sniff all my friends, and I will chase any dog who looks like he or she needs a good chasing.

Most of the other dogs in the park run after the squirrels, but I don't because we have had many different kinds of squirrels at Work, and I have learned they don't like to be chased. That makes no sense, but squirrels are squirrels and not dogs. Cats don't like to be chased, either, so they may be a type of squirrel. I'm not sure about that, though.

Being chased, or chasing, is one of the most fun times to be had, and it is not my fault if squirrels and cats don't understand this.

After chasing, I usually go over to the water bowl to get a drink. There is an enormous water bowl at the dog park for all of us to share. One time a dog named Boggs sat in the water dish. He is a big dog with a black face. I do not know why he thought he would be comfortable sitting in the water bowl, but once he did, the water smelled like Boggs and no one wanted to take a drink of it.

Fortunately, Maggie Rose came over and put in fresh water, so we didn't have to drink Boggs-water. We were all grateful for this, but we were nervous that Boggs might sit in the nice new water.

We tried to distract him by going over to the trees on the other side of

the park where the male dogs lift their legs and the females squat. At least, that's why I went and squatted there, so that Boggs would be lured to come over to examine the fresh scent. The other dogs may just have marked the area because I was doing it.

Anyway, it succeeded, because Boggs naturally needed to spend a lot of time sniffing all the trees and lifting his own leg, and then he had to leave with his person so he didn't have a chance to put his butt in the water bowl again.

I suppose people can sit in water bowls if they want, but I have never seen anyone do it. I've never seen any dog but Boggs do it, either. And he's an odd animal, anyway, because he never runs after a ball—not when it is thrown by a person, not when another dog has it in his mouth. He may not understand what a ball even is.

On the day that I made a new friend, I was in the far end of the dog park by myself. I like to go there sometimes and think about what a wonderful life I have. I get to go to Work. I get to play with all sorts of animals. There's the dog park and Maggie Rose. No one has a better life than I do.

Running along the back of the dog park, there is a fence that I can see through. Overhead, there are many trees that drop nuts on the ground. At the base of one of the trees, I saw a little squirrel. I knew that Maggie Rose called that kind of squirrel a *chipmunk,* but it sure looked like a squirrel to me. It hopped like a squirrel, ate nuts like a squirrel, and it certainly smelled like a squirrel. People make all the rules and can name things whatever they want, but to me, a squirrel is a squirrel is a squirrel.

The chipmunk was busy finding nuts and stuffing them into its mouth. There were so many nuts in there that its cheeks were puffed out in a very silly fashion. No dog would do something so silly, but squirrels have different rules—for one thing, they are allowed to climb trees. (I don't really like nuts. Some dogs do, but to me it's squirrel food. I would much rather have a meat treat.)

This chipmunk was so busy making silly cheeks with his nuts that he did not notice that there was a large hawk circling overhead.

At once, I became very concerned. I knew from doing work high up in the mountains with Dad that a hawk hunts lit-tle animals. I had seen hawks fly down and grab small crea-tures the

size of a chipmunk. Was this hawk flying around and around the little chipmunk because it was planning to hunt it?

I could not let that happen. Because the chipmunk was in the dog park, it was one of my friends. Maybe not a friend who would chase a ball or wrestle with a stick, but a friend just the same. I could not let the hawk hunt a friend.

But how could I stop it from doing that? Dogs cannot fly any more than we can climb trees. I wondered if I should bark, but my experience with squirrels of all kinds is that they don't care what dogs do unless we chase them.

But if I chased the chipmunk, that would not help because a hawk can catch a running creature. I stood frozen, afraid for my new little friend.

I was still watching the chipmunk and seeing that the hawk was coming closer and closer when suddenly the sky darkened, and I heard the flutter of many wings. It was a big mob of crows! They were all flying straight at the hawk!

It was just like when Bryan and Craig played football, which is a game where children run around with a ball and dogs are not allowed to help, even though putting in a dog or two would make it much more fun. I had learned from watching football that when a child is carrying the ball, the other kids will all chase him and jump on him. That's what the crows were doing now. They were swooping down and trying to grab the hawk with their beaks!

The hawk was clearly annoyed by all these big black birds that were flying around and pushing it and getting in its way. For some reason, the crows were trying to make the hawk fly away from the dog park and go somewhere else. Maybe there was a hawk park.

The hawk swooped and dove and changed direction, but there were so many crows pestering it, it finally gave up and flew away. The little chipmunk was safe!

Not that it was paying any attention. It was so busy digging for nuts, it had never once bothered to look up at the sky. That's just one of the many differences between squirrels and dogs: a dog always knows what is going on.

When the crows finally succeeded in driving away the hawk, the sky was clear of any birds. And that is when I saw Casey.

I did not know Casey's name at the time, of course. That would come later. All I knew was that I saw a crow hopping very strangely on the ground. One wing flapped, but the other one seemed pinched and pressed up against his side. There was something wrong with the crow, because they are supposed to fly, and this one could not.

Helping animals that cannot do what they are supposed to do is the most import-ant thing that Mom and Dad do at Work. Sometimes we help animals who are lost and hungry and just need a warm place and a good dinner before their family comes to get them. Sometimes the animals are hurt and need different kinds of help.

This crow seemed hurt.

I turned and looked across the dog park. Maggie Rose had been sitting on a bench reading a book, but now she was standing and looking at me. Maggie Rose is my per-son, and she can tell when I am upset.

I turned back to see what the crow was doing and noticed something amazing. The little chipmunk was hopping around with so many nuts in its mouth that they were fall-ing out of its cheeks! I guess chipmunks love making silly faces so much, they will keep stuffing nuts into their mouths until they are nearly ready to burst.

As I watched, I saw the little chipmunk scamper over to a hole under the fence and drop a couple of nuts on the way. That is when the amazing thing happened: the crow with the broken wing hopped over to the nuts, picked them up, and ate them.

I had found out a new thing: crows and chipmunks were friends! This made me happy. I like to make animal friends, too, but I don't eat nuts, so I did not go over to join in the shared meal.

I turned back to my girl and saw that she was coming toward me with a frown on her face. She saw the crow and put a hand to her mouth.

"Lily," she called, "what happened to that crow? Is it hurt?"

I wagged and sat, waiting for her to come help the poor bird. She approached slowly, so I knew that she didn't want to frighten the crow.

Now Maggie Rose was standing beside me. She knelt down and petted my head. "Good dog, Lily. That poor crow has a broken wing!" Maggie Rose held my head in her hand and looked into my eyes. "Lily," she said, "I'll go get Mom. You stay here and guard the crow. Watch him, Lily! Keep the crow safe!"

I did not know what Maggie Rose was saying, but I could hear concern in her voice, and I knew it had something to do with the poor crow. Also, she had said the word *Mom,* and I thought maybe what she was saying was that we needed Mom here to help with the crow and then later give me some treats from her pocket. Mom often had treats.

I was surprised when Maggie Rose turned and ran away. Did she want me to chase her? But the crow was clearly in trouble.

Maggie Rose passed through the double gate to the dog park and ran down the street toward Work. Where was she going? What was going to happen now? Why hadn't she taken me with her?

But I knew she would be back. Maggie Rose always came back, no matter what. While I was waiting for her, I decided I should make friends with the crow whose wing did not work.

I moved closer to him, but when I took a step, the crow hopped away. I took another step, and the crow hopped again. Even though

I am a friendly dog and everyone loves me, this crow seemed afraid of me.

This was ridiculous, of course. Cats are not afraid of me, horses are not afraid of me, and dogs are certainly not afraid of me. Even the little chipmunk hadn't been afraid—it had been so busy stuffing its face that it had paid me no attention at all. But this crow seemed to think I would hurt him.

With every hop, the crow was closer to the fence. When he reached the fence, I think he felt trapped. He turned and looked at me.

Now, if I went closer, the crow would have nowhere to hop. It would feel like being in a cage.

I decided that the best thing I could do was stop trying to catch up to the crow, just lie down and watch it. Maybe that way it would understand that I was Lily, a very nice dog who had many friends who were not dogs: cats, a ferret, kittens, and even a bunny rabbit.

Now that I was lying down with my nose pointed toward the crow, he was looking at me very closely. He kept turning his head one way and then the other.

I waited patiently, thinking this would be what Maggie Rose would want. She had never left me alone in the dog park before, so I figured out that I should not do what I usually did—chase other dogs and make sure that Boggs didn't sit in the water dish. Instead, I would watch this crow.

After some time of just staring at me, the crow with the broken wing took a hop in my direction! I decided it was a very young crow. It wasn't a baby, but it seemed smaller and somehow smoother than a lot of crows I had seen in the park.

The crow took another hop, then stopped

and twisted his head. I waited. The crow took another hop. Clearly, he wasn't just afraid—he also wanted to understand what I was doing there, just lying in the grass, not moving. Well, if it made him feel calm and curious, I was prepared to lie there all day.

The crow took another hop.

I waited.

With every hop, the crow flapped one wing, but the other one remained completely still, hanging by its side.

The crow took another hop. Another. And then, suddenly, the crow jumped up and landed right on my back!

Well, this was certainly a strange day. I had never seen a chipmunk feed a crow before. I had never seen a flock of crows save a chipmunk from a hawk before. I had never been left alone in the dog park before. And now, I had a crow on my back—something else that had never happened before.

When a crow is on a dog's back, the dog cannot easily fall asleep. However, the sun was warm, and I felt myself getting drowsy. Would Maggie Rose mind if I took a little nap while I was waiting for her?

My eyes may have shut, but they snapped open when I smelled something familiar. It was Maggie Rose! And it was the smell of Mom and Dad, too. They must have entered the dog park and were probably coming toward me because their scents were growing stronger.

I wagged, aware that I still had a crow on my back so I couldn't stand up and turn to face my human family. I hoped they would not think that I was being a bad dog. It was certainly a little embarrassing.

"Good dog, Lily!" I heard Maggie Rose call. That made it all right.

At the sound of my girl's voice, the crow jumped off my back and hopped back over to the fence, where it felt safe. Since I was back to being a regular dog and was no longer a crow bed, I stood up, shook, and ran to my girl and Mom and Dad.

Dad was carrying something that looked like a big handful of thin cloth. "It does look like a broken wing," he said. "We'll have to take him in and see if he can be saved."

"If he can be saved?" Maggie Rose repeated. "What do you mean, *if?*" I looked at her in concern. She sounded shocked.

"Well," Dad replied, "when a wild bird breaks a wing, it can be hard to repair. And this is a young crow, and crows are very social birds. I worry about keeping him at the shelter while he heals."

"What does it mean if we can't help him?" Maggie Rose wanted to know.

Dad was quiet for a moment. "Maggie Rose, we'll do what we can, but a bird with a broken wing can't survive in the wild. We'd have to keep him in a cage. I don't think he would be happy."

"But, Dad," Maggie Rose cried, "then we have to save him! He and Lily are friends! He was standing on Lily's back!"

"Well," Dad said, "we have to catch him first."

I watched as Dad shook out the cloth in his hand. It turned out to be a big square made of thin threads, all connected to each other so that it looked a bit like a spider-web. What was this game? I wagged, ready to tug on one end of the cloth if that's what we were doing, but then Mom spoke, surprising me. "No, Lily," she said. "Stay here with us."

I knew the word *no* and had never really liked it. But when Maggie Rose told me to do Sit, I obeyed her. Dad walked very slowly toward the crow with the damaged wing. I could sense Maggie Rose's heart beating in her chest, and she seemed afraid. I nosed her hand so that she would know that whatever was going on, her favorite dog in the whole world was right here, so it couldn't be that bad.

The crow was watching Dad even more closely than I was. The bird was back to twisting his head one way and then the other. In a sudden move, Dad raised his arms and flung the cloth through the air. The crow tried to take flight, but I guess it forgot it was hurt. It didn't even lift up off the ground.

Then the cloth landed on the crow, who flapped and fluttered while Dad stepped forward and grabbed the cloth and cinched it shut.

The crow squawked then, and I was sad because the squawk sounded so sad. Clearly, the crow thought something really bad was happening. I stopped doing Sit and went over to sniff at the cloth to try to make the crow feel better, but I could tell that it did not help.

Dad very carefully lifted the cloth, examining the crow. Mom walked over to look, too. Maggie Rose, however, came to me and rubbed her open hand on my head. "You are a good dog, Lily," she said. "You kept the crow calm."

I wagged at being a good dog for Maggie Rose.

"What is that around his wing?" Mom asked Dad.

Dad was tenderly turning the crow inside the cloth. "It looks like some sort of wire or string. It's so tight it's cut his flesh; can you see? I'm not sure what it is, but there are all sorts of wires and kite strings in the trees that a bird can get tangled in."

"Let's get this crow back to the rescue and see what we can do for the poor thing," Mom said.

When we arrived at Work, Dad carried the crow into a room, and I trotted off to see several of my newest friends. There were three little kittens in a cage I could not reach who were delighted to stand and stare down at me. They wanted to play, I knew, because on other days, Maggie Rose had let them out and we'd scampered around the room with each other. But today she did not do that.

Farther down the row of cages, right on the floor, there was an old dog named Brewster who thumped his tail but did not get up to greet me. Brewster was a brown, lazy dog who liked to take naps. He had been at Work longer than any other animal. Mom

sometimes called him a *senior dog,* which I suppose meant the same as *good dog* because Brewster was allowed to stay at Work so long.

"Brewster," Mom would say, "is going to be a challenge to adopt out. People want puppies more than they want senior dogs." I did not know what she was saying, but hearing her say *puppies* and *dogs* made me happy.

Brewster and I sometimes played together out in the yard, and one time we went to the dog park together, but for the most part, Brewster really liked to focus his attention on sleeping.

I greeted the other dogs and the adult cats in their cages and then went to be with Maggie Rose.

"Oh, Lily," Maggie Rose said, holding me tightly, "I sure hope Mom and Dad can save that poor bird."

The next time I saw that bird, he had a name and an outfit!

Maggie Rose and I went into Work a few days after I'd met the crow at the dog park. I smelled him right away, and Maggie Rose called out to him. "Good morning, Casey," she sang. "How's your wing today?"

Casey lived in a big wire cage with seeds on the floor and a stick he could hop on, sort of like a tree but with no leaves. He did not

have a blanket to sleep on, which might be why I never saw him lying down.

"Mom," Maggie Rose asked, "when will Casey be able to fly again?"

When she asked this question, Maggie Rose had been training me to do Roll Over. Roll Over is a complicated trick where a dog lies down on her stomach as if to take a nap like old Brewster. Then she lies on her back as if to get a tummy rub, and then she flops to the other side. I thought it was pretty pointless, but when I did Roll Over, Maggie

Rose gave me a turkey treat. I will do pretty much anything for turkey, pointless or not.

Mom was carrying a cat who had just arrived the day before. The cat was purring, which is what cats do instead of barking.

"Well, honey," Mom said, "we'll have to see if the operation was successful. If it was, then there's no reason why Casey shouldn't fly again. But we had to deal with some pretty deep cuts. We'll just have to wait."

I could feel that Maggie Rose was sad, so I went to comfort her by doing Roll Over without being asked. For some reason, there was no turkey for this.

With people, the rules change all the time.

Casey's outfit was a white coat that he wore on the wing he had been dragging. It smelled like cloth and a little bit like a strong chemical. His other wing still fluttered and stuck out, but he seemed to like wearing his new coat so much he never moved that wing at all. He let me sniff the coat, but I honestly didn't find it very interesting.

Casey and I were becoming good friends. I would visit him by going to his cage and sticking my nose against the wires every day. Casey would hop over to greet me.

One day, I noticed Casey watching Mom as she opened the cage door to put seeds in a bowl for him. After Mom had left, Casey went to the door of his cage and began pecking at it with his black beak. With a little bit of a rattle, the door swung open! Casey hopped out.

I bowed and wagged and jumped around in excitement as Casey hopped along the floor between the stacks of cages, saying hello to all the animals.

Casey was happy to see Brewster, who actually roused himself from a nap to wander over and sniff Casey from the other side of his gate. But Casey was far more interested in the kittens than anything else. He hopped up from one cage to another on the stack until he was off the floor, out of my reach, standing on top of an empty cage so that he could look right into the one with the three little kittens inside.

The kittens tried to reach out to play with Casey. They could stick their soft little paws between the wires to bat at him, but Casey was not interested in having them pet him on the head like a person would pet a dog.

Casey seemed to understand that kittens are not dogs, which is good information to have. A dog knows how to play by chewing very gently on a playmate, but kittens play with their claws. Sometimes they can accidentally hurt you. Adult cats are even more iffy when it comes to playing—some of them like dogs, and some of them despise dogs.

This makes no sense because dogs are wonderful, but it is true, just like it's true

that you Should Not Sit in the Dog Park Water Bowl. Casey was showing the proper amount of caution around the kittens, I felt.

When he made his way back down, one wing fluttering, he jumped right up on my back for a dog ride. I walked him around the room so he could see everything there was to see.

At first, it felt very strange to have a big black bird on my back, his tiny feet gripping my fur. But soon it started to feel ordinary. Casey liked to be up there—I think it made him feel safe. And I liked to have him up there because it was a completely new way of playing with another animal.

After taking a tour of all the cages, Casey hopped back up into his cage and then, reaching out with his beak, he pulled the door to his cage shut. I was very impressed.

We did this every day that I went to Work. Most days I was at Work because Mom or Dad had said the word *school,* and that meant Maggie Rose was gone for some time. Other days, though—the best days—were when Maggie Rose came to Work with me!

She would play with the kittens, she would play with Brewster, she would play with any puppies, and she would even reach her hand into Casey's cage, and he would hop onto her wrist and she would pull him out and talk to him.

One day, Mom came into the room while Maggie Rose was holding Casey. "Mom,"

Maggie Rose asked, "how is Casey's wing doing? Is it going to heal okay?"

"Well," Mom said, "we'll take his bandage off in another few days, and then we'll see."

"What'll happen if the wing didn't get fixed?" Maggie Rose asked.

"Oh," Mom said sadly, "I'm sure we'll figure out a home for Casey. But I think he'd rather be able to fly."

"I'd love to fly. Would you like to fly, Lily?"

I wagged, not sure what we were talking about but ready to play any game Maggie Rose came up with.

The next day when no one said *school*, Maggie Rose came to Work and watched while Mom removed Casey's coat. For the first time since I had met him, Casey flapped both of his wings! He didn't fly, though. He just sort of stretched his wings out.

Then Casey hopped down onto the floor and went over to visit the kittens.

"We still don't know if Casey can fly or not," said Mom. "Let's take him outside."

We all went into the yard together, and Dad came out to join us. I was happy that Casey was outside for the first time since he had come to live with us, because there are toys and grass and sticks out in the yard. I wondered what sort of games we might play together.

I hoped if I grabbed a ball Casey would do Chase-Me. That's a great game because I have the ball and everyone else wants it. Maggie Rose's brothers, Bryan and Craig, often played Chase-Me. But sometimes Craig was able to catch me and grab the ball, and then I had to play Chase-Craig, which wasn't as fun.

Casey hopped on the ground and poked a little at the dirt. I went and found a rope toy to see if he was interested in tugging on it, but he mostly just wanted to jump around.

"Can't he remember how to fly?" Maggie Rose asked anxiously, looking up at Mom.

Mom shook her head. "I don't know, honey. His wing may still be feeling sore or weak. I'm just not sure."

I felt the sadness coming off Mom and wondered if I should take the rope toy to her

to make her happy. Then Maggie Rose held out her hand, kneeling next to Casey. Casey hopped right up onto her hand. "Come on, Casey. You can fly," she urged.

Maggie Rose held Casey out at the end of her arm, but nothing else happened. I sat and scratched behind my ear, thinking that crow games are very different from dog games.

"Please, Casey. Please try to fly!"

Casey lifted his wings a little, and I stared at my girl, Maggie Rose, because both Casey and I could hear in her voice that this was important.

Crows can fly, and come together to mob hawks to protect their chipmunk friends, and hop over to see kittens. But as far as I know, they can't do much else. A dog, now—a dog can do a great many wonderful things if it just understands what is needed.

I decided that since Maggie Rose was holding her arm out, I should lift my paw, which is called *Shake*. It is a trick that Bryan taught me. He had hamburger pieces, so I caught on right away.

But nobody seemed to notice my Shake, even though I was doing it so well.

"I know," Mom said. "Maggie Rose, why don't you try running? Maybe the feeling of movement will give Casey the idea that he should try flying."

"That's a good idea," Dad agreed. "Maggie Rose? Keep your arm out and run into the wind."

I was startled and thrilled when all of a sudden Maggie Rose started to run, Casey still perched on her hand. Casey seemed excited, too, because he raised his wings. Maggie Rose ran around and around the yard. I chased her, holding the rope toy in my mouth so that this new game would be even more fun.

With a squawk, Casey flapped his wings. With a gasp of delight, Maggie Rose lifted her hand even higher. Casey flew into the air!

"Look, Dad!" Maggie Rose shouted. "Casey's flying!"

I sat with the rope toy in my mouth and watched as Casey soared far up into the sky. He flew in a big circle, flapping his wings. Maggie Rose was clapping, and Mom and Dad were smiling. Then Casey came gliding out of the sky and landed at Maggie Rose's feet.

I barked excitedly, dropping the rope toy in the grass. Then I jumped on it. We were all having such fun!

Dad turned to Mom. "Oh, boy," he said. "This isn't good."

Just like that, the joy left my human family, even though I was shaking that rope toy like crazy.

I hoped Casey understood what was going on, because I sure didn't.

That evening, I lay under Bryan's feet at the dinner table. Bryan will sometimes hand down a piece of dinner for me to snack on while I am lying there, waiting for everyone to finish and practically fainting with all the wonderful smells. Maggie Rose is my girl, but Bryan and Craig are part of the family, too,

so I love all of them. I love Bryan a lot if he is eating.

"I'm worried that Casey's become domesticated," Dad said. "That doesn't often happen with young birds, but he didn't seem to want to fly off. Maybe he's gotten too dependent on us giving him food."

"Maybe he just needs to find a crow family," Mom said.

"Yeah," Craig agreed, "like playing soccer. You can play by yourself, but it's much more fun with a team."

"Well," Bryan replied, "not more fun for Maggie Rose. She's such a little runt that no team would want her."

"That's just not a very nice thing to say, Bryan," Dad replied gruffly. "I think maybe after you apologize to Maggie Rose you should do the dishes for the rest of the week so you can think about what it would take for you to be nicer to your sister."

Bryan groaned and kicked his legs and did not feed me any more treats.

"Maggie Rose, you are such fun. Would you like to play ball with me after dinner?" Craig asked sweetly.

"Yes!" my girl said.

I jumped up. Ball?

Dad laughed. "Okay, that sounded pretty fake, Craig."

Then everyone laughed.

Except Bryan.

The next day was not a day where people said *school.* Instead, we went for a car ride! Dad drove, and Craig sat next to him. Casey was in his cage in the very back, and I was in the second seat with Maggie Rose and Bryan. The three of us in the second seat were mostly watching out the window for other dogs to bark at.

"Wouldn't it make more sense to release Casey up in the mountains?" Maggie Rose asked. "There are lots of crows up there."

"Good question, Maggie Rose," Dad answered. "But a flock of crows in the mountains is much less likely to accept a strange crow than a flock in the city. No one knows why, but I suspect it has to do with the birds all being more crowded here. The crows in cities are much more used to seeing strange birds. So we're going to take Casey to a big city park where I know there are lots and lots of crows hanging around, and I hope they accept him."

"But what if they don't like Casey?"

"Well, we can keep trying. Maybe we'll find another flock. Or Casey might just fly off on his own. Lone crows are not uncommon, especially males, but they're always safer in a group. Do you know what a flock of crows is called?"

"I know!" Craig called out.

"Let's see if your sister or brother knows," Dad replied.

Bryan rubbed his chin. "A crow flock?"

Dad laughed.

"I don't know," Maggie Rose admitted.

I saw a squirrel out the window and wagged.

"Craig?"

"A murder?" Craig replied.

Bryan laughed.

"Actually," Dad replied, "Craig is right.

A group of crows is called a *murder* of crows. No one's sure why. Maybe just because they'll surround a dead animal to eat it. But there are people who think that crows are evil and bring death."

"Casey isn't evil," Maggie Rose objected. "He's friendly!"

"I did a report on crows," Craig said. "They're smart. When a crow dies, the other crows will all surround him, because they're trying to figure out what happened. If it was an animal attack, they try to learn from it."

"Even I didn't know that," Dad said. "Very interesting. And that's another reason why it would be better if Casey joined a family— so that he could learn from them."

We went to a park! It was not the kind of park where dogs are allowed to run around without a leash. That made it not the best kind of park, but still, there were many smells and there were trees and there was a big pond—and I noticed there were a lot of birds.

There were big birds floating in the water, and there were little birds in the trees, and there were groups of crows that were on the ground poking at the dirt with their beaks. Dad set Casey's cage on the ground, and Casey was so excited he opened the door himself and jumped out.

"Wow!" Dad said. "I didn't know Casey knew how to do that!"

"You're a smart bird, Casey!" Maggie Rose called out.

Casey was obviously very interested in the crows that were across a big lawn. He kept looking at them, cocking his head to one side and the other, the way he had done when he first met me. After a time, he hopped up and flew a little bit closer to the big group of crows. They ignored Casey, probably not realizing what a special bird he was and that he had a dog for a friend.

Maggie Rose and Dad walked around pointing at birds, and Bryan and Craig threw a ball to each other. I decided to stick with the boys, and sure enough, Bryan dropped one of Craig's throws, and then we had a lot of fun playing Chase-Me-I-Have-Bryan's-Ball-and-You-Don't. Craig and Bryan kept yelling, "Drop it, Lily!" which I decided meant "Keep running with the ball, Lily!"

Eventually, I let the boys tackle me and take the ball out of my mouth. "Yuck," Craig said, "it's covered in dog spit!"

I wagged at the word *dog*. I trotted over to be with Dad and Maggie Rose because they were down at the pond watching the big birds float.

After a little while, I noticed that Casey had hopped closer and closer to the other crows. I wondered if he was making friends with them. I wondered if they would let me make friends, too.

The trouble was, I did not know any crow games other than the one where Casey would ride on my back. There were many, many crows, and I did not think I could hold all of them up on my back.

Then I saw a dog running across the park. It was a brown spotted dog who was dragging his leash.

"A springer spaniel," Dad said to Maggie Rose. "That's a bird dog. Bred to hunt birds with his owner. See how excited he is with all the birds in the park? He probably yanked the leash right out of his owner's hand."

I watched as the brown dog very rudely ran right into the middle of Casey's friends. They all took off into the air, Casey included.

They flew around the park in a big, open circle. And then they flew up into the air over the trees and went away.

"Beau! Come back here!" a woman was yelling. She had her hands on her hips, but the brown spotted dog didn't seem to know that meant he was being a bad dog. I knew, though, so I pressed against Maggie Rose's leg, being a good dog, and waited for Casey to return.

But Casey did not come back.

Dad called the boys, and we all went to the car. I noticed Maggie Rose had her head down, as if she were watching for something to happen on the ground.

When we got to the car, Casey was not in his cage. I realized then that he was going to stay with his crow friends. Maybe they would all find some chipmunks to play with.

I was very sad. Maggie Rose was my best friend in the world, but Casey was my best bird friend. I had not realized how much I enjoyed being with Casey until he left.

"I know you were sorry to see Casey go," Dad said to my girl. "But believe me, this is best. It's your mom's job and mine, too. We take care of animals, we help them get better when they're sick or injured, and then we release them back into the wild."

"Except puppies," Craig said.

"Right," Dad replied. "Dogs can't live in the wild, so your mom finds them homes."

"And cats," Bryan said.

"True enough."

"And monkeys!" Craig said. He laughed.

"Whales! Dolphins!" Bryan hooted.

"If I come across a whale up in the mountains, I will do my best to find it a good home." Dad chuckled.

Both boys were laughing, but Maggie Rose was sad. She could probably feel the emptiness in the cage behind us, just as I did. It felt as if Casey were still in there, but every time I checked, he wasn't. Casey was gone.

I hoped Casey would be happy with his new friends. But I was sure he would miss me, just the way I was missing him.

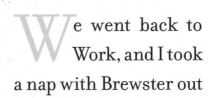

We went back to Work, and I took a nap with Brewster out in the yard while Maggie Rose helped Mom with the cat cages. I had a dream that Casey was on my back. Then I went in and took a nap with Maggie Rose on a narrow, soft bed where she liked to lie down sometimes, often with a book. She was still a sad girl, so I pressed up against her, letting her know that she had the love of her dog.

I was sound asleep when I heard a tap. I opened one lazy eye, wondering what I had just heard. Then there was another tap. This was certainly a puzzle. What could be making that noise? Should I get up and see what was going on, or nap?

Nap, I decided.

*Tap.*

I raised my head and looked around. Was someone knocking on the door? I did not think that was it. I yawned and started to put my head back down and heard it again. *Tap. Tap, tap.*

All right, time to figure out what was happening. I stretched, but I stayed on the bed so that another nap could be easily had if I decided whatever was making the noise wasn't worth investigating.

*Tap.*

I looked and saw to my surprise that a crow was standing on the window ledge,

tapping on the glass with his beak. It was
Casey! He was back!

*Tap.*

Maggie Rose seemed to be sound asleep, so I gave her face a lick. She kept her eyes closed but wiped at her cheek with her fingers. I licked her again. Giggling, she opened her eyes.

"Oh, Lily, you are so silly. Why are you kissing me right now?"

*Tap.*

Maggie Rose heard the noise. She sat up and frowned. Then her face brightened, and she gasped. "Look, Lily! It's Casey!"

We ran down the hallway and out the door into the yard. Casey was waiting for us. I circled the yard joyously while Casey flew over and landed right on Maggie Rose's outstretched hand. "Why are you here, Casey?" she asked. "Didn't you want to stay with your new crow family?"

Casey twisted his head back and forth at Maggie Rose's question, so maybe he understood it. Then he lifted his wings and flapped up into the air and glided over to the back gate. He turned and looked to us.

"What is it, Casey?"

The crow pecked at the gate. I wandered over to look through the wires to the other side, but I saw no friendly chipmunks or any other animals. Then Casey fluttered up to the gate latch and pecked there, scrabbling a little with his feet before dropping back down next to me.

"Do you want us to leave the yard?" Maggie Rose asked.

Casey just stared at her. I headed to the fence and lifted my leg like a male dog, which I do sometimes. I had never seen Casey do that. I couldn't fly like a crow, but I could mark the fence, which was probably more satisfying, anyway.

"Mom," Maggie Rose called. "Is it okay if I leave the yard?"

"Don't go far!" Mom yelled from some-where inside.

When my girl walked over to Casey, he fluttered up over the fence and landed on the other side of the gate. He came to the wires and poked his beak through so that I could sniff him. "Okay," Maggie Rose said, "I have no idea what we're doing, but let's go." Maggie Rose snapped a leash into my collar, and we went for a walk!

It was a very different sort of walk from those I had ever taken before. Casey was mostly on the ground and was hopping and holding his one wing the way he had the very first time I saw him. I remembered that I had followed him when he had been hopping like that, and now we were following him again. Did Casey remember the first day we met? Was that why he was hopping so strangely, so that I would track right behind him?

"Where are you taking us, Casey?" Maggie Rose asked.

I did not know what she was saying, but I thought perhaps she was asking Casey if his wing was hurt again. I hoped not. That would mean Casey had to wear a coat, and with that coat on, he was much less active and never flew anywhere.

Casey led us down the sidewalk, still hopping. Maggie Rose was confused; I could tell by the slow way she was walking.

I passed several yards where dogs had marked, and I wanted to stop and sniff each place, but my girl tugged my leash because Casey didn't know enough to wait for me to paint my own scent over the other dogs'. I liked Casey, but sometimes he could be irritating.

Casey flopped his way over to the base of a tree. Once there, he folded his wings normally. When we came closer, Casey crouched down. Then he started flapping his wings and rose up into the air. He landed in the tree right over our heads, and that is when I smelled it—there was an animal in that tree.

A kitten! Casey had led us to a kitten who was in the tree!

"Oh, my," Maggie Rose said. "There's a little kitten! It's stuck up in the tree! Come on, Lily. We need to go get help!"

Now we were running! I scampered joyously next to my girl. We ran all the way back to Mom's Work, leaving Casey and the kitten back in the tree.

When we got to Work, Bryan and Craig were playing with a big ball in the grass. I immediately ran over to try to take the ball away, and both boys shouted, "No!"

I still didn't like that word very much.

"There's a little kitten stuck in a tree!" Maggie Rose told them. "Can you come help? Casey found her."

"Casey's back?" Craig asked.

"Yes!"

I wagged that they were saying *Casey* so much, but I would have been even happier if they had let me play with the ball.

"Wait a minute," Bryan scoffed. "You mean to tell me the crow led you to a stuck cat? How is that even possible, Runt?"

"Yes, Casey did exactly that, and Dad said to stop calling me *Runt!*"

Craig picked up the ball and tossed it from one hand to the other. I watched, fascinated. "Okay, let's go check it out," he said.

The boys followed us back to the tree where Casey was sitting on a branch near the frightened kitten. Bryan and Craig kicked the ball back and forth all the way, but I didn't try to chase it because I was in no mood to hear them yell, "No!" again.

"Hey!" Bryan said. "The runt was right! There's a kitten stuck in that tree."

We all looked up to where the kitten was still cling-ing to the trunk of the tree with its little claws. It glanced down at us and opened its mouth and made a very tiny, "Meew."

"I can get it," Craig said. He went to the tree and hugged it. I watched curiously. Then he kicked his legs and hugged the trunk higher, inching his way up the tree.

Maggie Rose clapped her hands together.

I looked at the ball. Maybe I should grab it while Craig was up the tree.

Craig soon made it to the branch where Casey was sitting. He swung himself up, and Casey fluttered his wings a bit, moving over to make room. "The kitten doesn't have a collar," he called down. He reached out his hands, very gently pulling the frightened little kitten off the tree trunk. I could hear the ripping sound her claws made as they were lifted from the bark.

"I have no idea how this little thing got up here," Craig said down to us. "She must have been chased by a dog or something."

I heard the word *dog* and wagged.

Craig put the little kitten inside his shirt and then hugged the tree and slid back down to the ground. He reached up inside his shirt and pulled out the little kitten so that we could all smell it. Well, I smelled it, anyway.

Bryan and Craig and Maggie Rose took the kitten to Mom, who looked it over.

"She's well fed," Mom observed. "She's not a stray. We'll put up notices, and I'm sure her family will come claim her. She must have just escaped from someone's house. Good job saving her, Maggie Rose. And you boys, I'm proud of you."

"Don't forget Casey!" Maggie Rose said. As she spoke, there was a tap. We looked up and saw Casey standing on the window ledge, and he pecked again at the glass. He wanted us to join him in the yard!

Maggie Rose let me out into the yard, and Casey flew up and landed on my back for a dog ride. Mom came out to watch.

"Maybe we could have Lily put on a dog show to raise some money for the shelter." Mom laughed.

I wagged because they were both so happy.

"I could teach Lily tricks!" Maggie Rose said. "Would you like to be in a show, Lily?"

"When I was a little girl, I wanted to put on animal shows on TV," Mom said. "I trained my first dog to jump through hoops and sit on benches and thought someone would drive by and see me and make me a TV star. But what I do now is much better, saving animals every day. You, too, Maggie Rose. I'd rather have you here than on TV. I'd miss you."

"And I would miss Lily. Maybe we should just do our own dog show, here in the yard. Casey can ride Lily's back, and I could teach Brewster to do some tricks, too."

"That could be fun. I'm sure you could teach Casey, too. Did you know that crows are so smart they can learn to say actual words?" Mom asked Maggie Rose.

"What? They can talk?" Maggie Rose said. She sounded delighted.

"Well, they can't have a real conversation, but they can say a few words. When I was growing up, a man down the street had a pet crow who could say, 'I love you.' Only it had trouble with the letter *L,* so it would say, 'I ruv you.' Actually, it was more like, 'I ruv roo.'"

I wagged at Mom's voice, feeling Casey's hard little feet up on my back. Maggie Rose fell to her knees next to me. "Can you talk, Casey?"

I wondered if my girl was asking Casey if he wanted a peanut. Whenever Maggie Rose fed Casey, the crow seemed most excited about the peanuts, even though they were still in the shell.

I might eat a peanut if I had to, but really I'd prefer almost anything else.

"Lily?" Maggie Rose said. "*Lily? Say Lily,* Casey? *Lily? Lily?*"

I stared at Maggie Rose, absolutely mystified. What did she want me to do? Why was she saying my name? I looked around the yard, but I could think of no reason why she would be calling to me when I was sitting right here.

"Say *Lily*, Casey! *Lily!*"

Mom chuckled. "Well, I don't know how they learn words, so that might not work, Maggie Rose. But you can keep trying."

"*Lily!* Say *Lily*, Casey?"

Casey and I both stared at my girl. What on earth was she doing?

From that day on, Casey was back to being my friend. He might fly away for a day or longer, but he always came back to see Maggie Rose and me at Work.

That little kitten Casey found didn't live with us very long. In fact, it was the very next day when a woman came. She called the cat *Mittens,* and when Mom took the little cat from her cage to the woman, the woman started crying.

"I was sure I'd lost Mittens," the woman said, wiping her eyes. I could tell her feelings were very strong. Dogs have feelings, too, but mostly they are just happy ones, so we don't ever need to cry. "Thank you so much for saving her!"

"Well," Mom replied, "it was something of a group effort."

When the woman left holding the little kitten, I saw Casey high in the sky. The woman drove away, and Casey followed. I knew that Casey was making sure the kitten was safe.

# 10

Casey came back that afternoon, and we waited in the yard together for Maggie Rose to quit being at the place called *school* and come play with us. When the gate finally opened and my girl came in, I raced around the yard in a frenzy of joy!

Casey flew right up and landed on my girl's outstretched hand.

"*Lily?* Can you say *Lily*, Casey? *Lily?*" Maggie Rose asked.

That again. I went to Maggie Rose and did a very good Sit, thinking if I were the best dog I could be, we could end this crazy behavior.

Casey flew over and landed on my head.

I felt him up there, so I held very still. My girl giggled so hard she sat on the ground.

I wagged. Whatever we were doing, it was making Maggie Rose so happy she couldn't even stand up.

"Do you want to go on a picnic, Lily?" Maggie Rose asked.

I had learned that *picnic* meant that we would go to the dog park and sit on a blanket, and Maggie Rose would give me treats out of a basket. I very much liked Doing Picnic.

It turned out that Casey liked picnics, too. He came along to the dog park and flew right down to land on the blanket with us.

Boggs the dog came running over to see us, and Casey wisely flew up in the trees so that Boggs wouldn't sit on him. I was friendly to Boggs, but I watched him closely as he sniffed at the basket with food in it. Those were not his treats in there. I could smell my treats, my girl's snack, and peanuts for Casey.

Maggie Rose called Boggs a good dog, which to me meant she had forgotten about Boggs sitting in the water bowl. Sitting in a water bowl is bad dog behavior and is the sort of thing a dog would never forget.

Boggs ran off to do whatever he was doing, and my girl reached into the basket for the treats. Yes! She had a loop of flashy metal on her wrist. Dangling off this circle of wire were very small dog tags that glittered in the sun.

Casey found the thing fascinating, and he flew down from the tree to sit close to my girl and stare at the dangling dog tags, twisting his head side to side.

"You really like my charm bracelet, don't you, Casey?" Maggie Rose asked him. When Maggie Rose held out her wrist, Casey pecked cautiously at the dangling things.

"Here's a peanut," my girl said. I wagged so that the whole give-a-treat thing would continue—but hopefully with something other than peanuts. Casey took the peanut, which was fine by me.

"*Lily?* Can you say *Lily,* Casey?" Maggie Rose held out a peanut, the dog tags on her wrist glinting. Casey pecked at the flashing metal and took the peanut.

"*Lily?*" Maggie Rose repeated.

I was Lily, and I was right there waiting for my treat. Finally, my girl gave me one. It tasted like dried fish. I wagged, because when Maggie Rose handed me a treat, it meant she loved me. I was her dog, and she was my girl, and Casey was our crow.

As I was eating my treat, Casey flew away to peck at the ground. He came back to our blanket with something in his beak. It was a small glittery object a lot like what was hanging from Maggie Rose's wrist.

"Oh my gosh!" Maggie Rose exclaimed. "You found a charm, Casey! Thank you so much!" Maggie Rose took whatever it was from Casey's beak.

It did not look much like food to me, and so I sat patiently waiting for the topic of treats to come up. My girl fussed with this new shiny thing and then held out her arm—the object Casey had found was now dangling from the loop of flashy wire on her wrist. "Look!" she said.

I wagged, not understanding but happy, anyway.

Maggie Rose reached into the small basket next to her legs and pulled out a peanut. "Here, Casey," she said. "You deserve a reward for bringing me a charm."

Casey took the peanut with his beak and then flew up into the trees to eat it. He dropped the shells, which I found interesting.

The few times I had tried to eat peanuts, I crunched them up, shells and all. Then little bits of what tasted like wood sat on my tongue until I went to the water bowl, sniffed to make sure Boggs hadn't been sitting in it, and then lapped up as much as I could drink. But Casey knew how to open the shells.

A few days later, we did picnic again. This time, I noticed there were several crows in the trees.

None of them came down to see us except Casey, of course. And Casey had something in his mouth. Maggie Rose laughed as she accepted it from him. "Why, Casey, this is so nice of you. It isn't really a charm. It's a dime. But you deserve a reward just the same."

Maggie Rose gave Casey another peanut, and he flew up into the trees. Some of the crows made noises at him. Crows cannot bark. They can only make a loud call that probably is their way of saying they wish they could be dogs.

A little while later, Casey returned with yet another glittery object. Maggie Rose laughed and clapped her hands.

"Casey," she said, "this is wonderful! Let's see what you've got here. Oh! You brought me a tiny bell from a cat collar. This would make a very noisy charm, so I won't wear it, but it's beautiful just the same. Here, Casey." Maggie Rose handed over another peanut from the basket.

Casey looked at me, perhaps to see if I wanted it. But I was waiting for a piece of cheese and had no interest in crow treats.

After cheese, I played Chase-the-Brown-Dog with a dog named Pete, and then several dogs played Chase-Lily-She-Has-the-Ball with me. I drank more water and then plopped down next to my girl, who was eating an apple and holding an object called a *book*.

A book is a dry thing that my girl often stared at as if it were about to come alive and run around. I chewed up a few of them when I was a puppy and found that they tasted even worse than peanut shells.

So now I flopped on my back, my legs in the air, thinking that doing a half Roll Over would earn me another piece of cheese, but Maggie Rose didn't even notice. She never looked up from her book until Casey flew down with something in his mouth, another small, glittery object.

"A bottle cap!" Maggie Rose exclaimed. She gave Casey a peanut. I found the whole process boring, but I stayed on the blanket because I smelled a wonderful slice of meat in a sandwich in the basket.

Then something very alarming happened. When Casey flew up into the tree to drop his peanut shells, another crow landed on our blanket.

Maggie Rose and I held very, very still.

I didn't dare move. I knew that crows who are not Casey are often scared by dogs, and I didn't want to scare this new crow away before I had a chance to make friends with it.

Indeed, this new crow was very nervous. Its legs were bent, and it seemed ready to take flight at the slightest movement.

"Hello there, Mr. Crow," Maggie Rose greeted it very softly.

The crow had something in its mouth. It perched on the edge of the blanket, giving Maggie Rose one of those twisting-head looks that it must have learned from Casey.

"Did you bring that for me?" my girl asked. Maggie Rose very carefully and slowly reached into her basket and brought out one of Casey's peanuts. "That's a metal washer. My dad has some in the garage. I'm sure he'd like another one. Would you like a reward for bringing it to me?" The crow dropped the metal thing from its mouth and bounced forward a few hops and very cautiously removed the peanut from Maggie Rose's fingers.

I followed the crow's flight as it rose up into the trees and realized that all of its crow friends were up there watching this whole thing.

"It's a murder of crows, Lily," Maggie Rose breathed. "And look how many of them are carrying something in their beaks!"

I wagged because she had said my name and because of the smells that came out of that basket when she lifted the lid.

It wasn't long before two more crows had landed on the blanket, each with small, glinting objects in their beaks. Maggie Rose started giggling. "This is so much fun!" she exclaimed.

I was pretty discouraged that picnic had stopped being about pieces of sandwich for a good dog and was now all about the strange crows who kept flying down to land on our blanket, drop metal objects, grab peanuts from Maggie Rose's fingers, and fly away.

This was not how picnic was supposed to be played!

It was, I decided, Casey's fault. None of this would have happened if he hadn't given Maggie Rose a small piece of metal. I never made him try to play one of my games, yet here I was stuck in an endless game of Crows Landing and No Sandwich for Lily.

Soon (much too soon because I had not yet been given a treat), Maggie Rose stood up and folded up the blanket we had been sitting on. "Let's go tell Mom about this!" Maggie Rose said.

Dismally, I followed her out the double gates, sniffing sadly at the basket that was swinging at the end of her arm. My girl had put all the trinkets in that basket. She could have pulled something for a good dog *out* of the basket. But today was all about crows, apparently.

"Look, Mom," Maggie Rose said once we

arrived at Work. "I told you about how Casey was bringing me charms and coins and other little pieces of metal and I was giving him peanuts. Now all the crows are doing it!"

Mom shook her head, using her finger to sort through the worthless trinkets the crows had given Maggie Rose in their effort to ruin the game of picnic.

"Crows are amazingly smart animals," Mom said. "But, Maggie Rose, we can't let them depend on people for their food. We need to untrain this behavior in the crows."

"What do you mean, Mom?"

"Well, like a lot of intelligent animals, crows will do whatever they can not to have to work too hard."

"Like Bryan?" Maggie Rose asked.

Mom laughed. "Maybe. So if you're in the park handing out peanuts, the crows may start thinking that instead of going off to forage for other food, they should just hang out and wait for you to come back. And then what happens when you can't get to the park every day? The crows are thinking, 'Maggie Rose will come back! We don't dare leave the park and miss out on all the free peanuts!' So instead of flying off to find food, they stay there, waiting for you to feed them, getting hungrier and hungrier. At some point, the crows might get so hungry they become sick."

I could see that my girl had lost all of the happiness she had gained at the dog park. I nudged her hand. I knew she'd feel happier if she just remembered to give me a treat.

"I'm sorry, Mom."

"Oh, don't worry, sweetheart. I don't think this has gone on long enough to do any real harm."

The basket was still up there on the table. I wondered if what they were talking about was the best way to give me what was left of Maggie Rose's sandwich.

"What do I do now?" Maggie Rose asked.

"You should take all of these little gifts back to the park and set them on a blanket with you so they can see them. And then don't accept any more trinkets. Even if they drop them right in front of you, don't reward them anymore."

"Not even from Casey?"

"Not even Casey. The other crows will see you feeding him, and they can be pretty stubborn; they'll keep bringing you items until they get another peanut from you. As far as they're concerned, you're feeding all crows, not just your friend Casey."

"Come on, Lily," Maggie Rose said.

We went back to the dog park with the basket and the blanket! It appeared we were going to try picnic again. This time, I sure hoped that Maggie Rose got it right.

# 12

We sat on the blanket, and Maggie Rose spread out all the items that the crows had brought. I do not know why the crows picked up things like that in the first place. They are not even good to eat.

Immediately, Casey and some of his crow friends landed on the blanket, each with a glittery thing in its beak. I yawned, already bored with the game. I wandered a few steps away and started sniffing at the ground in case anybody had peed there.

I could hear Maggie Rose speaking from behind me. "I'm sorry, birds," she said. "I can't reward you anymore. You can't start to think of me as a way to get food."

The crows hopped around, the trinkets in their beaks. They also looked carefully at all of the glittery items that Maggie Rose had spread out on the blanket, turning their heads one way and another, probably thinking we would all be better off if Maggie Rose would just reach into her basket and give me a piece of her sandwich.

Since there was no sandwich, I picked up a bit of stick and shook it hard. I'm very good at shaking things.

"Do you understand?" Maggie Rose asked. "I brought these back to show I don't want them and won't give you any more peanuts. I'm sorry, but that's what Mom said to do.

Please don't be angry. Please just fly away. Then I'll know you understand. Fly away, crows. Please?"

The crows flapped and hopped and made their dry, croaking noises. I shook the stick even harder, and to my surprise, it flew out of my mouth, heading straight for our blanket.

The stick landed right in the middle of the crows' trinkets. Maggie Rose jumped in surprise, and I raced for the blanket. This was so exciting! It was as if I'd thrown a stick for myself to catch. I bet I was the very first dog who ever managed to do anything like that.

The crows were startled when I leaped onto the blanket and snatched the stick up in my teeth. They flapped up into the air and scattered into the sky. Casey went with them.

I noticed that when the crows landed on the tree branches, they dropped the trinkets from their mouth. The little shiny things fluttered to the ground like peanut shells. The birds all stared down at us with obvious disapproval.

I flopped onto my belly and began to chew my stick into bits.

"Oh, Lily, good," Maggie Rose said softly. "You got them to leave! I think they understand now. They won't be back for more peanuts. Good, Lily. Good dog!"

I was so happy that I was a good dog. I was so happy to feel Maggie Rose's hand on my fur as she stroked my back.

In a minute, I felt something else on my back as well. Casey had landed there. The crows in the trees stared down at us. Probably they had never seen a crow with his own dog before and were wondering how to get one for themselves.

After a while, one by one, the crows flapped away. It was just Casey who was left on the blanket with Maggie Rose and me.

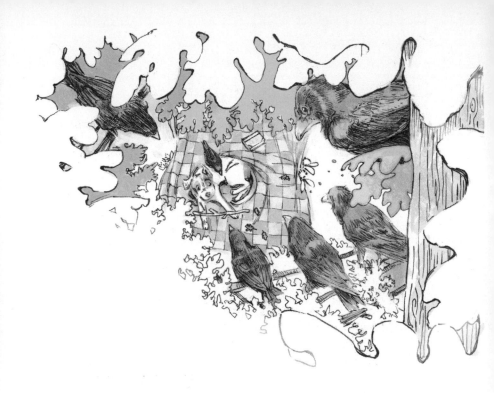

Casey hopped off my back and drew close to Maggie Rose. My girl picked something up off the blanket and held it out to him. "Here, Casey," Maggie Rose said. "I can't give you any more peanuts, but I can give you a charm in case you ever decide to make your own bracelet!"

Casey looked at the thing in Maggie Rose's pinched fingers. Finally, he reached out and snatched it from her hand and flew into the trees.

"Well, Lily," Maggie Rose said to me, "I think they got the message. But it makes me sad. They were just trying to bring me charms, and they probably feel like I didn't like any of their gifts. But I did." She sighed.

"Working in animal rescue is hard, Lily. It seems like it would always be fun, but sometimes you have to clean out the cat cages, and sometimes you have to do something you don't want to do like let an animal go or give a puppy you love to a new family."

Maggie Rose seemed a little sad, so I stopped chewing my stick and nudged her with my nose to let her know that the best way to be happy was to give a dog a bite of some of the sandwich in her basket. I started wagging furiously when she reached inside the basket and pulled out a small bag, which

she opened, letting the marvelous smell of her sandwich into the air.

"Not you, though, Lily. I won't ever have to say good-bye to you."

Just then, Casey fluttered back down and landed on the blanket. I would have to call this bad timing, because Maggie Rose let the hand with the sandwich drop back into the basket. No!

Casey no longer carried the gift that Maggie Rose had given him in his beak. But he had something, and he hopped over to her and offered it.

Maggie Rose laughed happily. "Oh, look, Lily! I gave Casey the charm, and he is rewarding me!"

It was a peanut.

I sighed in disgust.

Maggie Rose took the bag out of the basket, broke off a little piece of sandwich,

Ree-Ree

and gave it to me. At last! Casey watched her feed me.

"Can you say *Lily,* Casey? *Lily?*"

"Ree-ree," Casey croaked. "Ree-ree."

Maggie Rose gasped. "You did it! You said *Lily,* Casey!"

There was so much joy in her voice that I wagged as hard as I could. We were finally Doing Picnic the right way.

## MORE ABOUT CROWS

American crows (like Casey) are known as *corvids*. Other corvids include ravens, magpies, and rooks.

Corvids are among the most intelligent birds. Some have been seen using tools. They might poke sticks into trees to search for food or put nuts on roads for cars to crack.

Crows and other corvids can be trained to say words, just as Maggie Rose trains Casey to say, *Lily*.

A female crow lays four or five eggs at a time in a nest that is between one and two feet across.

Crows sometimes bring objects to people, just as Casey and the other crows bring gifts to Maggie Rose. A girl in Seattle began feeding neighborhood crows peanuts and pet food in her backyard, and the crows brought objects back to her—a button, a paper clip, bits of broken glass.

Crows seem to recognize and remember people they don't trust. Some researchers wore masks when they trapped crows to study them. After the crows were released, they made a scolding call to alert other crows to danger if they spotted anyone wearing those masks.

Crows will eat almost anything from seeds, nuts, and fruit to eggs and small animals. They will even grab chicks from other birds' nests to eat.

In the winter, crows sometimes gather together in groups called *roosts.* The largest roosts can have up to two million crows!

Crows sometimes crush the ants and rub them into their feathers. Chemicals in the ants' bodies may keep other insects or parasites away from the crows. It's a bit like spraying themselves with insect repellent.

If a crow dies, other crows may surround it in what is called a *crow funeral,* just as Craig tells Maggie Rose. They seem to be trying to figure out how the crow died.

# ABOUT THE AUTHOR

W. BRUCE CAMERON is the *New York Times* bestselling author of *A Dog's Purpose*, *A Dog's Journey*, *A Dog's Way Home*, *A Dog's Promise*, and the young-reader novels *Bailey's Story*, *Ellie's Story*, *Lily's Story*, *Max's Story*, *Molly's Story*, *Shelby's Story*, and *Toby's Story*. He lives in California.

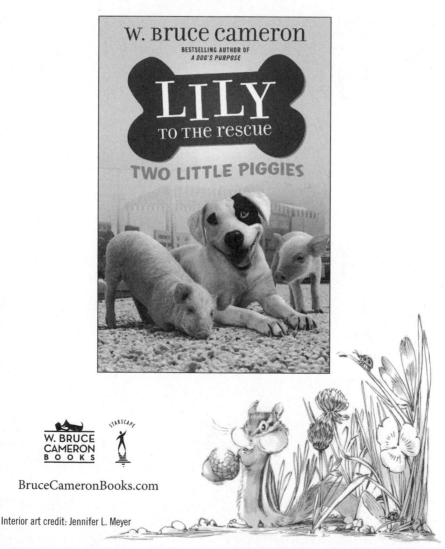

READ ON FOR A SNEAK PEEK
AT *LILY TO THE RESCUE: TWO
LITTLE PIGGIES,* COMING SOON
FROM STARSCAPE

Where are the pigs, Mom? Are we going to a farm?" Craig asked.

Mom shook her head. "No," she replied. "It's the strangest thing. I just got the call. It may even be a hoax. They said that there are two baby pigs running around inside a truck stop off the highway. It doesn't seem very likely, but that's what they said."

"What's a hoax?" Maggie Rose asked.

"It's kind of a joke that involves someone telling a lie," Mom replied.

"Well, then," Maggie Rose said, "I hope it's not a hoax because I'd love to see some little piglets. Can I name them, Mom?"

"We'll see," Mom answered.

"If they're boy pigs, then Craig and I should name them," Bryan declared.

"We'll see," Mom repeated. I wagged because I smelled wonderful things outside the car, things like dogs and trees and horses and other animals. Wherever we were going was probably going to be a lot of fun!

We drove long enough for me to become drowsy in the backseat and fall asleep with my head on Bryan's shoulder. When he said, "Lily, quit breathing on me," I woke up a little and licked his ear. Everyone laughed but Bryan, so I did it again.

Bryan had eaten a peanut butter sandwich earlier and I could taste it on his ear, which I thought was simply amazing. Why don't all people put peanut butter in their ears? It seemed a very smart thing to do.

I licked Bryan's ear again, and he pushed my face away.

Finally we arrived at a hot place where the ground was covered with hard cement and the grass and trees were in the distance. Nearby, cars and trucks large and small roared up and down a very busy road.

"Okay everyone," Mom said. "Stay close to me. I don't know what we're dealing with here."

We walked up to some glass doors and when they slid open a gust of cold air brought me delicious food scents: melted cheese, broiling hot dogs, sweet sticky drinks in cans and cups.

There was something else as well: two animals I had never smelled before. There were animals inside this place!

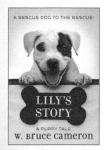
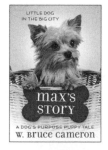
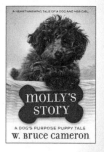
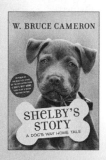
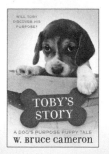